SHOT THROUGH THE HEART

A FAERIE TALE

by

C.A. King

Cover Design: Just Write Creations

Editor: J.D. Cunegan

This book is dedicated to everyone who has ever felt as if they were stuck between two places.
May you find the one you were meant to be in.

Look for other books by C.A. King, including:

The Portal Prophecies:
Book I - A Keeper's Destiny
Book II - A Halloween's Curse
Book III - Frost Bitten
Book IV - Sleeping Sands
Book V - Deadly Perceptions
Book VI - Finding Balance

Tomoiya's Story:

Book I: Escape to Darkness
Book II: Collecting Tears

Surviving the Sins:

Book I: Answering the Call
Book II: Pride
Book III: Lust

When Leaves Fall: A Different Point of View Story

Peach Coloured Daisies: A Cursed by the Gods Story

Flower Shields: A Four Horsemen Novel
Drawing Strength From Words: A Four Horsemen Novel

Miracles Not Included

Twisted Tales of A Dead End Street

Cover Design: **Just Write Creations**

First Printing: June 2018

ISBN: 978-1-988301-42-6

Kings Toe Publishing
kingstoepublishing@gmail.com
Burlington, Ontario. Canada

CHAPTER ONE

A twitch of the nose wasn't enough to prevent red from overtaking its rounded tip. Normally, only an oncoming sneeze would cause such a colour to appear. Adelia wiggled her ears. That didn't help, either. The rosy tint of the blush simply covered them as well. She glanced over her shoulder at the clips binding her wings and sighed. She was, for all intents and purposes, a criminal until proven otherwise. The problem was, not even she was convinced of her innocence.

Two guards dressed in silver sandwiched her as they walked down the long narrow hallway. This was the walk of shame stories were told about. Pictures of the most despicable offenders her world had ever known lined the walls - a reminder of the harsh hand of justice that ruled with an iron fist. The guards paused at each one so she could fully comprehend the seriousness of the situation. This was the difference between being a faerie and ending up known as a fairy - a term no respectful member of society even muttered out loud.

Her eyes avoided contact as much as possible, but curiosity won the battle. There were no names to indicate who she was looking at. It wasn't necessary. Everyone knew who had fallen from grace.

The first was Mordescius, posing with a full view of his notoriously broken teeth. That mouth was the reason for his downfall. The rest of his appearance wasn't much better. He wore a grey undershirt, showing off every detail of the absence of care for the rest of his body. Adelia could almost smell the lack of cleanliness wafting out of the picture. Unshaven stubble and a cigarette hanging from the corner of his lips, he was the definition of disgrace. Faeries didn't smoke. That was a human shortcoming. Of course, faeries also didn't bribe children for their teeth.

On Mordescius' first trip to the world of men, he'd noticed young mortals had two sets of teeth, one of which fell out on its own. Faeries only had the one set and those couldn't be repaired. If something happened to any of them, they needed to be replaced. Unfortunately, there weren't any extras lying around to replace them with. The new world he'd been introduced to had plenty to go around.

The Consillium weren't ones to begrudge a citizen a few teeth. It was the way Mordescius went about it that was the problem. A faerie's number one law was not to interact within the world of men. There were jobs to be done, but in secrecy. The fallout of having been seen in true form lasted for eternity. That was exactly what Mordescius ended up being sentenced to do - live his immortal life as a byproduct of active human imaginations. He was dubbed the Tooth Fairy and spent his time leaving bits and baubles in exchange for children's teeth.

The rest of the pictures were of those just as infamous. Each had fallen under the cold grip of addiction's right hand. Sugar was the drug of choice, being more harmful to a faerie than the hardest drugs to a mortal. The end result was a string of once respected do-gooders banished to live as fairy godmothers, each messing up and fixing their mistakes over and over in a never-ending nightmare. They were the junkies of the faerie realm. She recalled the story of one so high on sweets, she actually tried to use a pumpkin as a carriage. Such acts were horrible but dulled in comparison to the one who ingested so much of the powdery substance that she kidnapped a bunch of children from their beds, dragging them across several worlds before being caught.

The guards halted at a set of large marble doors. The two simultaneously reached up with one hand, grasping a golden knocker. In unison, they swung it back then pushed it forward with force, starting a chain reaction of noises. A symphony of birds singing ended with the doors opening inwards. Her escorts parted to the side, motioning for her to continue on alone.

The sound of a lock turning told her she was sealed inside the chamber along with her fate. She squinted. The room was whiter than a first snowfall. The top of the Consillium's bench hovered feet above her head. She'd heard glancing up was like staring directly into the sun's most powerful rays. The group proceeding over her today were three of the elite. It was said their wings had been touched by angels, giving them a glow of gold more beautiful and dangerous than anything any faerie had seen before. She dared not attempt to steal even the slightest peek.

"Adelia, faerie of the cloud realm Watchovia," a voice bellowed louder than necessary. "You have been accused of breaking our most sacred law. How do you plead?"

Adelia glanced at each of her feet. Her lips twitched from side to side. With a shrug of her shoulders she responded, "I'm not sure."

"You aren't sure?" Another voice echoed from above. "Do you deny consorting with mortals and directly interfering with their lives?"

"Yes, I suppose I did that," Adelia admitted. "But with reason."

"Reason?" the voice repeated. "What reason could there be to break the law?"

"I'm not sure it's that cut and dry," Adelia said, biting her lip afterwards. Nobody argued with the Consillium. "Perhaps there should be some allowances in the law."

"How dare you!" a deep male voice yelled.

"Now, Quissum, let's not be hasty. I'd like to hear what she has to say. Perhaps there is a good reason why she should be allowed to violate a law that has been in place for thousands of years."

Adelia gulped back the saliva pooling in her mouth, wondering if her heart was beating double time or if it was simply loud enough to echo throughout the chamber. "Thank you," she said, glad to have at least an opportunity to explain. "It all started when I was promoted..."

CHAPTER TWO

"I expected a few more," Adelia said, glancing at the empty chairs around them.

"You act like it's an easy task, going from imaginary friend to the cupid department," Junapree answered. He scratched his nose, making his left ear twitch. "The others simply weren't good enough... not like us."

"You always did think highly of yourself," Adelia replied.

"And of you," Junapree said, slouching back in the chair. He crossed his legs, taking his own advice that one might as well be comfortable any time one had to wait.

Waiting was exactly what the pair were doing. It was the season of love in the world of men and the cupid department was understaffed. That was the reason for mid-year promotions in the first place. It wasn't that there was a decline in faeries, but rather an increase in the non-magical population causing the problem. The cupid department was spread thinner than a bald man's hairline.

"Good afternoon," a middle-aged faerie said. A stereotypical cupid she wasn't. Wearing a black suit with her hair tied back in a tight bun, she resembled more of a regulatory officer than anything else. Lines had hardened into deep ridges on her face, as if the weight of the world had been carried by her for years. "I'm Eelbright, your de-briefer. I don't have time to dilly-dally or repeat myself, so the two of you best pay attention and take notes."

"Yes, ma'am," the two new recruits said in unison.

Adelia scrambled to open her books, sending paper scattering down, littering the ground around her. She offered a nervous smile accompanied by a shrug of her shoulders. "Sorry," she mumbled, knowing no one cared enough about her to give it any thought. Her ears began to burn, a red blush forming at the tip. Twitching them only sped up the process, spreading the colour faster.

Eelbright shook her head. Her eyes rolled upwards, as if calling on the heavens for help. "This is the best you could come up with?"

"Best they had," a voice boomed back, making it obvious it wasn't a higher power she was talking to, but rather another faerie who happened to be watching them from a higher position.

Perspiration wasn't normally a problem in the faerie world, yet here Adelia was feeling droplets starting to form on her brow. There was no warning for the sweat that formed on the back of her neck either. Her long dark hair simply drenched to the point of it being noticeable. Her hand made a circle of golden dust in front of her, before turning palm side up underneath it. The hoop solidified, falling into her cupped hand. It was the perfect accessory to tie back her hair. It wasn't pretty, but at least it held the stands off her neck.

"Great," Eelbright winced. "This one's got making hair ties for little girls down to perfection." She turned away, rolling her eyes.

"I was hot," Adelia complained.

"Hot?" Eelbright repeated. "You were hot?"

"Yes..." Adelia stuttered.

"You don't know the meaning of hot!" Eelbright bellowed. "But you will. That is a promise. There will be no more interruptions. Are we clear?"

"Yes, ma'am," the two recruits answered.

"Forget about being friends to children. Your training there won't help you here. Things are much more lenient when dealing with the young. Your number one law is not to fraternize with those living in the world of men. Is that clear?"

"Yes, ma'am."

"Good," Eelbright said, pacing in front of the two. "Your job is to shoot arrows of love, bringing two people together. That is done from a distance."

"Yes, ma'am."

"Please don't repeat that after every sentence I say," Eelbright complained. "It's annoying and unbecoming of a faerie working in the cupid department."

"Yes, ma'am," Adelia said, realizing afterwards Junapree had remained silent. The droplets doubled in size, trickling down the side of her face, following her hairline.

Eelbright sighed. "Stick to your jobs as assigned. There is to be zero deviation. If you do that, you will have no problems. You can follow instructions, can't you?"

Adelia bit her top lip to stop herself from speaking. She nodded.

"Yes, ma'am," Junapree said.

"Well, at least one of you is on the ball," Eelbright said.

Adelia's smile fell, the weight of disbelief pushing the corners of her lips down. The instructor was shaking Junapree's hand. All that was offered to her was a stern look and the beginnings of a scowl. The next few days were going to be the worst she'd ever lived through.

CHAPTER THREE

A crackling noise was the first thing to grab her attention. Golden sparkles formed a cloud above an equally shiny pot in the centre of the room that housed it. The mist over top rendered her speechless, yet content. Magic was in the air - literally. There it was bound to remain. Enchanted dust held no gravity. This was true power - stronger than the contents of a witch's cauldron on Halloween and more potent than the mischief of a thousand pixies.

The assignment room was bustling with faeries. Each waited in line for their turn to reach into the golden pot that contained the swirling magic. Inside lay not only their futures, but the lives of two non-magicals as well. All the mojo present was there for only one purpose: to bring the cupid department their specific assignments for the day. Once instructions were received, faeries bustled off to be outfitted. It wasn't clothing. Their outfits were no more special or unusual than every other day. No one was going to see them. It was all about the equipment - finding the right bow and arrow for the job.

Falling in love wasn't a simple matter. If anything, it took a lot of planning and involved many departments. Attraction in the world of man wasn't considered an abnormal thing. Lust, after-all, was a non-magical condition. Mortals were known to be a physical race. An arrow of love could change burning desire into a budding relationship, laying the foundation for it to bloom into something beautiful. On the flip side, for couples already matched, that very lust threatened to interfere, even destroy the whole process.

Emotions were a disease and a contagious one at that - a plague specific to the world of men. That was why different arrows were needed. Each produced distinctive results, based on whether they were creating or mending a relationship. Some were stronger than others. Beyond that, the one thing all faeries in her department needed to know was a single heart could only handle being shot a few times.

Math wasn't her strong point, nor was understanding equations. This one wasn't hard to grasp, though. There was a number no one person could exceed. Every arrow had its own value. The total of all arrows used on a single person had to remain less than the one assigned to them.

The pools in Adelia's eyes swirled, taking in everything. She spent an entire night memorizing each weapon available in her romantic arsenal. Knowing was half the battle. Picking the right instrument to fulfill her job and using it properly was the rest.

Her hand plunged into the swirling metallic colours, returning with a piece of paper. A rotating ray of light caught one corner. A band of brilliant colours exploded through the hovering mist. For a fleeting moment, she was at both ends of a rainbow, the promised prize lying in the palm of her hand.

"Move along," a voice ordered.

If anyone didn't know it was her first day before, they did now. She chuckled under her breath at the traffic jam she was solely responsible for. The line behind her had tripled in size. Almost as quickly as the paper disappeared into her pocket, she scrambled off, letting fate choose the direction.

The flow of the next room could have bested the white rapids of any fast-flowing river. She was merely a pebble caught in the speed with hundreds, if not thousands, of other tiny stones being forced along by nature's ire. Adelia felt panic rush through her veins - a dagger's sharp tip heading straight for her own heart. She could have been anyone or no one... it didn't matter which.

Faeries don't have emotions. Feelings like this are reserved for the world of men. Her own thoughts stung with the mal intent of angry hornets forced from their home. She drew in a breath and with it strength - a process she'd gone through a thousand times before and would likely need to perform a thousand times more.

Her hands curled into fists at the first bump against her shoulder. Not moving fast enough made her nothing more than a bouncing ball, ricocheting off the walls of the co-workers who surrounded her. Love might have been the end game, but there wasn't any where she stood. The corner of her eye caught sight of dimly lit cubicles to her left... against the flow.

Hands, legs, shoulders, chests, she felt them all nudging her the opposite way. Her arms swung out in front of her chest, pushing through the crowd. Their forward momentum became a propeller, launching her towards the little rooms and sanity. Once within her stride, she threw everything she had into making the final play, tossing her own body over the remaining obstacles. The crash on the other side hit hard, knocking her breath away. It was well worth it, though. In a few minutes she recovered and began to figure out her next step.

Her hand, still shaking, dove deep into her pocket, retrieving the instructions she'd received earlier. Two names were the sole words: May Jensen and Ricky Sage.

CHAPTER FOUR

There were two ways to enter the world of men. The first was the easiest: a simple flight down a tunnel of light. Faeries kept their magical forms intact - each cloaked in a magical illusion. The other was to take the form of a non-magical and live amongst them. For the cupid department, the first was all that was necessary or technically allowed.

Get in. Get out. That was the entire plan. How hard could it be? She stepped onto the platform and closed her eyes, hoping no one would see. It would have been an eternity of jesting if anyone found out she was the sole faerie afraid to look down. Heights weren't supposed to terrify those who could fly. If there had been anything around, maybe a rope to hang onto or a pole, it wouldn't have been as awful an experience. Magic wasn't tangible. There were no walls, ceiling or floor to this elevator. Truth be told, there wasn't even a door. A simple step off a cloud and then a descent at speeds that could make one's head spin like they were possessed by a demon.

Adelia's wings fluttered a little too late. Her feet touched the surface, tripping over each other, sending her tumbling to the ground. If she had timed it just right, she would have caught the updraft and floated away gracefully. Instead, she ended up in a heaping pile.

After a few deep breaths, she looked herself over for damage. There was nothing permanent, other than noting she was a bunch of D's, which didn't stand for breast size: Disgrace, Disastrous and Disappointing. It might have been a new exit point, but the trip was one she had made thousands of times - only a handful of which had been successful. That alone was proof that practice didn't always make perfect. Those words were part of the P's. All the letters had their own place in her life, good or bad - a little game she'd made up while being an imaginary friend.

Brushing off the negativity and her clothes, she glanced around. It made sense that she had been sent to a small town. Those jobs were significantly less complicated. Without the hustle and bustle of a big city, it was easier to hit a target without incident. Now, all she needed was May Jensen and Ricky Sage in the same place at the same time.

"Here goes nothing," Adele said, opening her hand in front of her face. Her lips puckered, blowing a kiss into the wind, silver sparkles carried within it searched for a bit of luck. The next time the wind blew, it changed directions, returning with a message. A flyer hit her, making an outline of her face in advertizements. She peeled it off.

Winter Blues Weekly Dine & Dance

Saturdays - Ricky's BBQ Barn after 7 pm

If there is snow on the ground we'll be heating things up.

Come join in the fun.

She blinked twice at the picture of two pigs dressed in farmer costumes and dancing underneath the words.

"Hm," she hummed. "I suppose this is target Ricky Sage. Looks like I am heading to a dance."

Time and faeries weren't two words that went together. The magical world didn't normally bother itself with seconds or minutes. Once down from the skies, there was no choice but to do exactly that. Everything in the world of men revolved around it. Their lives were measured by it. One was born, became a child, turned into an adult and then grew old. That was where love came into play. These beings had such a short amount of time in their form, spending it with someone else became important. Love made up for what time had stolen from them.

An expert she wasn't, but from looking around at the position of the sun and the activities of the mortals wandering around, it had to be afternoon. The absence of children, together with an increase of thirty-something women jotting about, meant schools were still in session for the day. That she'd known from her previous job. By early evening, the streets would be almost bare, with the exception of the occasional person or two. Traffic wouldn't pick back up until between seven and eight at night. When that happened, she'd be good to go. All she needed now was to figure out where Ricky's Place was - not an easy task when she couldn't ask anyone directly.

CHAPTER FIVE

Adelia crossed her arms over her chest, leaning her side against the building between two bales of hay, their golden hues catching what was left of the early evening sun's rays. Ricky's Place hadn't been as difficult to find as she anticipated. Whoever Ricky was, he'd managed to bring the rural into urban. Being the only barn in town made it stand out. It was an interesting gimmick in a world that prided itself on technological advancement. This place took a leap backwards, transporting folks to the clean country living of the past. Having solved the problem of locating where to be, she moved on to a more difficult task... getting inside. That was a bit more complicated.

As an imaginary friend, a child expected her to take a seat and participate in tea parties or other games. Those events were usually blamed on youthful imagination. As a faerie, that was the only department allowed to have interaction with mortals, mainly because as children grew, their memories of past happenstances became somewhat skewed. There were plausible reasons for disbelief. That wasn't the case for adults. She couldn't simply grasp the door handle and fling it open, especially on a day with no wind. Someone else had to open the door for her to enter. Then her timing needed to be spot-on. Being invisible didn't mean she wasn't taking up space. Bumping into nothing and feeling it was even worse for a mortal than seeing things move on their own. The non-magical needed explanations for everything.

She heard the ping of displaced stones. A cloud appeared, kicked up from the tires of an old pick-up truck heading towards the parking lot. Ricky's place bordered the business district, as little as there was, of the town. Still, it managed to keep its turn-of-the-century farm look, with handcrafted wooden fences lining a long dirt and gravel driveway, complete with pot holes. The driver paid no attention to them, the vehicle bouncing over each as if every street was meant to have them. She almost expected to hear a *yee-haw* followed by a wave of a cowboy hat. That thought was probably a by-product of watching too many cartoons at her previous job.

Adelia eyed the truck as it came closer. This was her chance. Whoever was arriving would be heading inside and she meant to follow. Her breath ceased as the vehicle took a sharp turn, heading directly for her. There was no time to move and even if there was, dust framing her outline would have been a dead giveaway as to her existence. She sucked in her gut, eyes clenched closed, waiting for impact. The engine purred, then let out a roar, backfiring as it came to a stop. A foot closer and it would have pinned her to the wall she rested against.

One eye pried open in time to see a man heading to the door. Keys jangled in one hand as he balanced a bag full of bottles in the other, trying to find the lock.

"Damn," he said, "just open. I don't have the time or patience for this tonight." He yanked on the door, putting his back into the struggle.

Adelia watched him repeat the process from all sides before figuring out what the man was trying to do. The key had to be turned while the door was pulled for it to open. Shrugging her shoulders, she decided to help. There was just enough space above the man's hand for her to hold on as well. She pulled as he turned. She staggered backwards as the door flew open without strain. Taking less than a second to regain her foothold, she barely managed to stop the door from closing, sneaking in as the lights turned on.

The scents of wood and whiskey mixed with the musty odour of straw that had seen one season too many filled her nostrils. It wasn't a pleasant smell, yet she found herself inhaling deeply as she surveyed the room. What were once wooden stalls used to house animals now were outfitted with tables and benches for friends to gather for an evening of fun. To one side, a raised platform acted as a stage for musical instruments. Beams and poles had all been replaced with newer materials, varnished to bring out the natural hues, each mark in the wood having its own story - one only the tree it came from knew the ending to.

The floor beneath her feet felt soft, not as plush as carpet, but smoother than one might expect from wood. A square section stood out. It was pale compared to the rest of the room, as if the traffic flow had been a hundred times busier there than anywhere else. Unlike a real barn, there wasn't a speck of dust to be found.

The man exchanged his jacket for an apron with a tag that read, Ricky. He was one part of the equation waiting to be solved. Adelia moved closer, watching his movements. A white cloth ran across the surface of a bar. She'd seen parents use less care cleaning their children. A glimmer in his eye told the story of a man in love - not with another person, or even a pet. This was a love she hadn't seen before. He loved this place and his job. For a moment, she questioned her assignment, but then who was she to judge what had been decided? She jumped on a stool and observed as he made preparations for the evening.

CHAPTER SIX

The smell of beer washed out any previously noted scents. The barn, now packed to capacity, held the garbled mix of dozens of conversations, each one struggling to be heard over top of live music and stamping feet. The crowd was both young and old. Here age didn't matter, as long as one was legal to drink alcohol.

A row of girls stood side-by-side at the bar, twirling strands of their hair and pretending to be a little more drunk than they actually were. They took turns ordering, each wanting their own chance to eye Ricky up and down as he fetched everything from wine to water. The amount of flirting taking place before her eyes progressed as the evening went on. With so many women interested, it was going to be difficult to figure out which one was May Jensen.

Adelia remained to the side, watching every move Ricky made, amused he wasn't giving even the slightest indication of interest in any of his admirers. He was a rock and built like one. There was an undeniable appeal that surrounded him, from his well-formed muscles to the warmth found in the brown shade of his eyes. A twinkle in them synchronized with the appearance of dimples each time he laughed at a terrible joke or shook hands with a patron like a long lost friend.

The heat of a thousand stares amassed on her back, scorching through to her core. A quick glance over her shoulder found her gaze locked on a woman weaving a path through bodies towards the bar. She leaned over top of it, flinging her long black hair to one side. A fresh gloss of red on plump lips glistened in the light. Raising one finger, she curled it, summoning the barkeep. This woman knew what her best assets were and wasn't afraid to show them off to the world.

A royal blue dress hung off her shoulders, clinging to every curve she owned. A light giggle was her reply to Ricky's fixation on the cleavage she'd hung out for display.

"I'll have a white wine, doll," she said.

"You got it, May," Ricky said, putting up a glass and fetching a bottle from the fridge. "Full or half?"

"Full," she answered, her lips wearing a pout. "If I have too many, you might have to drive me home. You don't mind, do you?" She sat back on a stool, folding one leg over the other in a manner to best show off high heels adorning dainty feet.

"I got this," the man on the stool next to her said, his eyes glued to the bronze tone of her skin. "My treat, little lady."

She forced a smile in his direction, holding up her cup in the motion of unsaid cheers. "Thank you," she mouthed, rolling her eyes in the bartender's direction.

Adelia shook her head. This was May. There had to be a mistake. Ricky had passion for what he did; for life. This woman was one step off from being a...

Her hand slapped over her mouth. Her thoughts stuttered. It wasn't the position of a faerie to judge. She had no right, nor should she have the inkling to question an assignment.

Taking in a breath, she pulled the arrow back on the bow, her hands shaking. The release was easy. The emotions that assaulted her afterwards were another matter. Watching the bartender, his face drained of all colour. It was as if her actions had sucked all that was good about this man right out of him and replaced it with something he couldn't have wanted. Disgust crawled over her skin. Why had she been tasked with taking away what someone loved and replacing it with something they didn't?

It was as if her persona had split into two. One was bound to do the job she had been assigned. The other felt for the man behind the bar. That part of her didn't want to shoot the second arrow. Both struck a chord within her, screaming their desires to be heard the loudest. Only one was able to claim victory. She stamped her feet on the ground, indecision her enemy.

"Darn it!" Adelia mumbled.

The arrow released, whizzing its way to the intended target, striking at the same time as another, one much larger than her own. Adelia spun around, looking for what she had missed while lost in her own preoccupation with the bartender - a second faerie.

"Junapree!" Adelia yelled. "What are you doing?"

"What am I doing?" Junapree echoed. "What are you doing? This is my target."

"No," Adelia argued, yanking him by his arm to an isolated corner. "May Jensen is my assignment." She pulled out the crinkled paper from her pocket. "See! May Jensen and Ricky Sage."

"Humph," Junapree grunted, retrieving a paper of his own. "See! May Jensen and Dean Sage."

"Well, they can't both be right," Adelia replied. "Wait! That says Mary, not May! You shot the wrong woman."

Junapree rubbed his chin. "Oops."

"Oops," Adelia snarled. "That's all you have to say? What was the second name, Dean Sage? Hang on. Are the two related?"

"How would I know?" Junapree complained. "I wasn't sent to study the family history. My job was to shoot the arrow and let them figure it out. I've done that."

"But," Adelia whined. "We can't both finish our assignments the way things are."

"No, we can't," Junapree snorted. "The bigger arrow trumps. I guess I win."

"This isn't a game," Adelia cried. "What will happen to the barkeep? He has already been shot. We have to make this right."

"And how do you plan on doing that?" Junapree asked, rolling his eyes. "It's done. I don't know what happens to your guy, but there is no fixing this."

"We need to tell someone what happened," Adelia demanded. "Someone must know what to do."

"And who do you plan to ask?"

CHAPTER SEVEN

Adelia poked her head around the corner, giving her a full view of the problem department. Her hand, tightly latched to Junapree's wrist, tugged hard enough to drag him along.

"Quickly!" she ordered. "There isn't anyone in there."

"Who do we have here?" An elder faerie asked, his nose as crooked as a goblin's. It twitched and sniffed, then twitched again. "New to the department?"

"Yes," Adelia answered with a half grin.

"Come to report a job well done, I hope," he said.

"Not exactly," Adelia replied.

A book twice the size as the desk it sat on slammed closed. The faerie giggled. It wasn't a sound of amusement or even happiness. This was a nervous chuckle born from fright. "Sh," he hissed, holding a single finger to his lips. "Follow me." He hopped down from a stool that stood three times higher than his height.

Adelia covered her mouth, trying to stop a gasp from escaping her lips. That would have been rude, even if she had never seen a dwarf faerie before. They were as rare as pygmy pixies and it had taken them twice as long to get the same rights. Rumours were always swirling about a group that had formed based on the belief a dwarf couldn't perform jobs as well as other faeries.

"Excuse me," Junapree said. "Where are we going?"

"To my office," the dwarf answered. "I want to congratulate the two of you on a job well done. Well done indeed." He glanced over his shoulder, sending an over exaggerated wink - an order for them to remain silent. "Here we are." Keys jingled as he detached them from his belt. "Come in. Come in." The door slammed behind them.

"Sir..." Adelia started, stopping at the sight of the dwarf banging his own head on the desk.

"One moment," he said, slamming his forehead down three more times. "Now, you two listen to me. Eelbright is already in a snit. The last fellow that messed up a job today was sent packing right down to troll duty."

Adelia crinkled her nose. Trolls were the most disgusting creatures to exist, even if they were the work horses that mined fairy dust. They ate almost anything and wore only loincloths to allow excretions to happen whenever and wherever they happened to be. Cleaning up after them was the worst job a faerie could be assigned to.

"She went to fix the problem herself and left me in charge," the dwarf continued. "If there are any problems while she is gone, I'll be knocked down there with you. So you see, everything needs to be fine."

"But," Adelia stuttered, "It's not fine. We have a real problem."

"Then you need to fix it!" the dwarf ordered.

"We would," Junapree explained, "but we don't know how."

"I see," the dwarf said. "Okay, tell me what it is and we'll put our heads together to come up with an answer."

"We were sent to the same town," Adelia started.

"With different targets," Junapree added. "Who were related and happened to have similar names."

"I see where this is going," the dwarf said in a matter-of-fact-tone. He spun around in his leather chair, his feet not even reaching to dangle off the end. "One of you shot the wrong person."

"Yes!" Junapree exclaimed.

"Well, that's an easy fix," the dwarf answered. "I take it this was a first time for these parties." He waited for the two to nod. "Then get a bigger arrow and have a re-do."

"Except," Adelia explained, "Junapree already used a larger size and I used a smaller one. The numbers aren't there to shoot again."

"Why in the clouds on a first timer would you do that?" he asked, throwing his arms in the air. "Bigger sizes are used for fixing. Didn't anyone explain that?"

"Actually, no," Adelia replied.

"Goodness sakes," the dwarf complained. "Who was the shoddy fool who trained you? I'll be giving them a piece of my mind..."

"Eelbright," Junapree interrupted. "Eelbright was our trainer."

The dwarf's face went white. He gulped back his words. "Well, I can't very well blame one of the department heads, now can I? Look, today is a bad day. Move on to a new assignment and we can revisit the problem later. I think that's best."

"What will happen to the man?" Adelia asked.

"What man?"

"The one I shot that doesn't have a match," Adelia stated. "What happens to him?"

The dwarf shrugged his shoulders. "Nothing. A new arrow should have appeared in your arsenal. Check now."

Adelia reached behind her back and pulled out a red arrow.

"That's it," the dwarf stated. "He'll live. There might be a bit of depression until the arrow finds someone for him."

"We can't leave him like that," Adelia barked back. "It's not ethical."

"Alright," the dwarf replied. "You said there were two couples. Find the other woman and crisscross the two."

"What if that doesn't work?" Adelia asked.

"The only other option is to find a new love for this mortal," the dwarf explained.

"How do we do that?" Junapree asked.

"One of you will have to go in undercover," the dwarf answered.

"You mean in mortal form?" Junapree questioned. "That isn't allowed."

"Neither is messing up your first assignments, but you two managed to do that quite fine," the dwarf replied. "While one is finding out who would be a good match, the other will have to hold down both of your assignments. I know it sounds daunting, but it will be fine. Just remember not to take too long or get too close to the subjects."

"What happens if we do?" Adelia asked.

"You risk becoming more mortal than you want to be. Emotions are contagious and that disease isn't something either of you want to catch. There is no cure."

"I'll take double duty," Junapree offered.

"Hand him your weapons," the dwarf ordered. "I'll take care of the paperwork. You'll have a home, everything you need and a backstory within the hour. Make sure you memorize every detail. You cannot be found out. If you are, we'll all be up on charges. Get in and get out. That's the plan. Stick to it."

"Funny," Adelia muttered. "I think I heard that plan once before."

CHAPTER EIGHT

The safehouse was made for mortal convenience, containing everything Adelia could have possibly needed. Even her closet was filled with clothes in all the right sizes. She took a gander at the contents of various cupboards and drawers, trying to make sense of what all the items were for. Her crash course in the world of men didn't include how to live as one of them.

Shrugging her shoulders, she made a decision. If she was to truly understand this world, she needed to dive right in. A pinch of glittering dust fell, sprinkling over top of her head. It cascaded down, transforming her body from faerie to mortal before its magic was spent and all that remained was a thin layer of dirt. In thousands of years some poor troll would be tasked with digging up the particles, the magic having renewed over time.

Adelia's new body wasn't what she had imagined it would be. She'd taken for granted having wings and the lightness of magic feet. Mortals were bogged down. A heaviness ruled over every inch of her - every movement requiring an energy she wasn't used to producing. It was a puzzle. Why did people put clothing over top of an already burdensome form? Still, she did, afterwards plopping down on the couch with her eyelids drooping and a new appreciation for the life mortals lived. She inhaled, feeling the weight of the air filling her lungs and then leaving again.

A newspaper lay open on the table before her. Adelia motioned for it to move to her, but nothing happened. In this form, everything had to be done without magic. That meant physically picking things up. Grumbling to herself, she moved it close enough to her face that she could read the small print. Apparently, as a non-magical person, her eyesight left something to be desired. As bad as they were, they still managed to catch a help wanted ad for Ricky's Bar. She might not have wanted a job, but at least she had a reason to talk to him and hopefully find out about the missing woman who should have been paired with Dean.

Pockets had always fascinated her. For as long as she could remember, she wondered about why they existed and what purpose they served. Looking at the array of items she needed to carry with her, she finally understood. Each one was designated with a purpose: keys; currency; identification; and a rectangle communication device she didn't have a clue how to use. She stashed it in a back pocket, intending to forget it existed.

She was finally ready to leave, but felt more like sitting down than doing anything else. Still, the sooner she completed her task, the sooner she could revert to being a faerie again. She locked the door behind her and set off down the road.

A burning sensation radiated from her legs into her lower back. Muscles that hadn't been used for an eternity screamed their displeasure at the sudden onslaught of activity. Her pace slowed. A dryness overtook her mouth and throat - a new uncomfortable sensation to bear. The bar coming into sight made things worse. She didn't know the pain in her legs could increase, but it did. The faster she tried to move, not only did it hurt more, but other things started to happen - frightening things. Her heart beat faster and heavier. Her breath laboured. Using a sleeve, she wiped beads of sweat from her brow. How did beings of this realm exist on a daily basis?

Fingers eagerly gripped the handle, pulling the door open. She took a moment to compose herself before waltzing in, pretending all was right in the world.

"Hello?" Adelia called out.

"We're closed," Ricky said. He tilted his head back, drinking every last drop of liquid a shot glass had to offer, before pouring another.

"I'm here about the job," Adelia explained, waving the newspaper in the air.

"Great," Ricky replied, sucking back another drink. "Come back tomorrow. We are closed for a funeral today."

"Funeral!" Adelia echoed. "Did someone die?"

Ricky poured another shot. "That is usually why we have funerals," he moaned. "Anyways, I'm not taking applications today."

"Okay," Adelia conceded, heading for the door. She stopped short of leaving, changing directions at the last second. "Are you okay?"

Ricky side-eyed her, letting out a snort. He kicked the chair opposite him out from under the table. "Have a seat."

Adelia accept his offer, watching him pour two shots instead of one. He nudged a glass in her direction, lifting the other in the air. "Cheers."

"Were you close to the deceased?" Adelia pried.

Ricky huffed. "I thought I was going to be." He knocked back another shot. "She was supposed to marry my father. He'd picked out the ring and set the date. They were going to make it official."

Adelia gasped. If he was talking about Mary, there was a new kink in their plans. But why would she be dead?

"You are probably wondering what happened," Ricky said, his speech starting to slur from the alcohol. "As I said, they picked the date and planned an engagement party. Mary, that was her name. Mary wanted her daughter to be in town for the big event." He reached for the bottle, swearing under his breath when it produced only a couple of drops. "Are you going to drink that?"

Adelia shook her head, not knowing what to say.

"Where was I?" Ricky asked. "Oh yeah, Mary's daughter. She shows up all pretty like and I think we are hitting it off. We were spending time together and getting kind of cozy, if you know what I mean. I was going to talk to my father about her. I mean, I didn't want anyone feeling weird about me dating my step-mother-to-be's only daughter." He tried to pour another drink from the empty bottle. "Did you drink the rest?"

Adelia shook her head. "So what happened?"

"What happened?" Ricky repeated. "I'll tell you what happened. My old man left with her. I thought he was giving her a ride home... being a gentleman. Then I find out the truth. Do you know how I found out?"

"No," Adelia admitted.

"Mary keeled over in the coffee shop down the road," he continued. "They said it was a heart attack, but I know it was a broken heart. She'd told the whole room she'd found her daughter in bed with my dad."

"That's terrible," Adelia sympathized.

"You think that's bad, guess who is wearing the ring," Ricky said, shaking a finger in the air. "That's right... May is wearing the very ring that was bought for her mother. Mary is dead and I'm left out in the cold."

"Maybe you can find someone else," Adelia suggested. "There must be other women who have caught your attention."

"Nope," Ricky said. "I've sworn them off. No more love for me." His head fell like a lead weight banging on the table.

CHAPTER NINE

"So, did you find Mary?" Junapree asked.

"Yeah," Adelia said. "About that... she's dead."

"Dead?"

"Long story," Adelia replied. "All that matters in the end is we cannot use her as a crossover. It is a worse situation than I thought." She fell back onto the couch, sinking in. Nothing could have felt better than peeling off socks after wearing them all day. Her eyelids blinked, trying their best to remain open.

"How so?" Junapree questioned. "The challenge is still the same: find the barkeep another mate. At this point, it doesn't matter which one. I say we go to that bar; blindfold me; and I let an arrow go. Whoever it hits, it hits."

"Have you lost your mind?" Adelia shrieked. "This is a man's life we are talking about - his heart. Don't you care what happens to him?"

"No, I don't," Junapree admitted. "And the fact that you do is worrying. We are faeries. We don't have mundane emotions. You've been here less than a day and you already sympathize. The sooner we get this over with, the better."

"I'm not going to pick someone out of..."

"The pot?" Junapree interrupted. "That is exactly what we do without question on a daily basis. We don't know if the slips of paper are right and we don't go looking into every case to make sure they are. It's all a shot in the dark, nothing more."

"No," Adelia blurted out, her hands covering her ears. "It's magic. Whoever or whatever picks those names knows what they are doing. I have to believe that. There is greater purpose for each of us. What's the sense in existing if there isn't?"

"I don't know," Junapree admitted, shrugging his shoulders. He sighed. "I'll give you another day to figure out who gets the arrow. After that, I'm taking the shot myself."

Adelia opened her mouth, but a low grumble escaped rather than words. "What was that?" she asked, glancing around the room.

Junapree shook his head. "You are in mortal form now. Eating and drinking isn't just for pleasure." He nodded in her direction. "That body requires sustenance to survive." He snapped his fingers, an apple appearing, suspended in front of him. He snatched it up, lobbing it across the room.

Adelia's reflexes weren't quick enough. "Ow!" she complained, rubbing her head where the fruit made contact.

"Heads up," Junapree said, chuckling. "I forgot mortal reflexes aren't as nimble as the magical. Eat that; you'll feel better."

She hadn't needed the invitation. White teeth were already making their way past the shiny red skin. A soft crunch followed. The sudden burst of sweet juices took her by surprise - a mouthful of ecstasy. For that moment, as brief as it was, nothing else mattered. It wasn't long enough. Her mouth returned for a second bite, taste buds demanding more.

There was something about apples that had always intrigued her. It was the one food faeries couldn't taste. They were considered the forbidden fruit, although she didn't understand why. There were no stories about it - no warnings. It simply was something faeries could not experience. Now, in mortal form, she could.

"You remembered," she mumbled, her mouth still full.

"How couldn't I?" Junapree said, rolling his eyes. "You went on about it for an entire century... apples this, apples that."

"Mm," she hummed. "It's so good. I wish you could taste it."

"That's the thing," Junapree replied, "I don't. I don't have any inkling to try anything the world of men has to offer. We have more than they could ever hope for - magic."

"Maybe," Adelia said, finishing the last bite of the apple. She examined the core, seeds still intact. "Do you think this would grow if I planted it?"

"Listen to yourself, Adelia!" Junapree exclaimed. "It doesn't matter if a seed becomes a tree. We can make apples at the snap of a finger. We can grow an orchard at the blink of our eyes. Why are you even contemplating that core as anything more than garbage?" He snapped his fingers, the remnants of the apple disappeared, shiny dust scattering down in its place.

"That was rude," Adelia snapped. "I was just curious. We may have magic, but we weren't the ones who created life. That is something none of us should take for granted."

"I'll be back tomorrow," Junapree said. "Have it worked out by then. I'm not risking my future on a single mortal man. I suggest you don't either."

CHAPTER TEN

Adelia's eyelids had minds of their own, opening ever so slightly then drooping back down. Her mortal form refused to give up that fleeting moment that existed only in the shadows that lay between the dream realm and reality.

Her senses took turns awakening from slumber. Everything was a new sensation, no matter how big or small - good or bad. Sleep wasn't something she'd given much thought to. It simply wasn't relevant before. Now it was. As bothersome as she had found being tired to be, if she hadn't experienced it, she wouldn't have understood the feeling of waking up to a new day. There was a sense of achievement that attached itself to the realization a new day of possibilities had begun.

Her tongue explored the cavern of her mouth, dried out and screaming for even a trickle of liquid to soothe the feeling of sandpaper scraping against an uneven surface. That was enough to start her moving.

She let the tap run. Water cascaded over her fingers. She relished the feeling every drop made, slowly numbing her fingers to a chill. Her palate refused to wait any longer. The glass filled only part way before moving to her mouth. The first sip was pure luxury, moisture coating lips, teeth and tongue. A cool sensation travelled to the back of her throat. making its way down.

Adelia examined the glass, a new realization forming in her mind. She'd always wondered how mortals handled bad experiences. Now she understood. Going through hard times made the good things feel so much better. It was the combination of the two that made being alive worthwhile. A smile crept over her lips. She'd done more living in one day as a mortal than in centuries as a faerie.

Grooming was another task she needed to perfect. There was a lot of effort that went into appearances in the mortal land. She grasped the end of a hairbrush tightly, pulling it through knots that had formed overnight, wincing as strands of hair broke from the pressure. The air that had been trapped in her lungs during the process escaped in one large huff.

A buzzing noise interrupted the next stroke. She spun around, looking for wherever the noise was coming from, and finding nothing. It sounded again, and this time she felt a vibration radiating through her lower spine.

"What magic is this?" she cried. "Junapree, if you are playing tricks on me, it isn't very funny."

The vibrations continued at regular intervals. Her hand smoothed over her backside, feeling the pulsing as she came to the pocket. It dove in, retrieving the communication device that had been provided to her.

She tossed it on the table, watching it jolt around as if it had a mind of its own. Suddenly there was silence, not just in sound, but movement as well. She peered over top of the device, anticipating a ploy to catch her off-guard. A sudden ding made her jump back again. It took several minutes for her to find enough courage to explore what had happened. Still, she needed to know what the signals meant. It was a crucial aspect of surviving in the world of men.

The round circular button captivated her attention; locking her in a battle she couldn't win. There was a better chance of beating a cyclops at a staring contest than not pressing that one spot. A single finger stretched out, inching closer. Curiosity had taken a hold and only satisfaction could save her.

The screen lit up at a single touch, displaying a message. *Where are you? You are late... Ricky.*

"Eek!" Adelia squealed, slamming the door behind her. The note she left on the table beside Ricky had completely slipped her mind. Time wasn't something she was used to worrying about. Everything was far more intense when magic wasn't involved.

***

The walk to Ricky's place might have been easier if it hadn't been for the fact she'd been moving at twice the pace as she had the day before. A minute outside the door wasn't going to be enough to regain control of her breathing. Any longer than that, however, would have negated the time advantage she'd sacrificed her body for.

"Sorry I'm late," she huffed, sliding into a booth across from him.

"Did you run here?" he asked.

"I did," Adelia admitted, the pink in her cheeks starting to give way to pale skin. "I don't drive. It's not that bad when I'm not in a hurry." That was a lie. A tidal wave of guilt hit her dead on, knocking her down and refusing to let her back up again. She had a new emotion to deal with. This one wasn't a toy to be played with. It had a name - one she'd heard before but paid no attention to - a conscious.

"Are you okay?" Ricky asked, side-eyeing her.

"I am," she grimaced at the spew of untruths flowing from her mouth. It was uncontrollable. "Are you okay?"

Ricky chuckled. "You mean because of yesterday? Pft. I was just letting off some steam. Don't pay attention to anything I said." His eyes remained fastened to the papers in front of him.

Adelia examined his posture and attitude. He was lying just as she had and she understood why. Mortals didn't want people to know the bad stuff. They didn't want to be pitied. It was easier to pretend to be fine than to admit one wasn't.

"I'm sorry," Adelia mumbled.

The pen fell from Ricky's hand, rolling to the edge of the table. His eyes slowly moved to meet hers. "There is nothing to be sorry for."

"There is," she argued. "What happened to you isn't right and it isn't easy. I'm sorry it happened to you. You deserve better."

"I appreciate that," Ricky replied, offering an obviously fake smile. "It's not like you had anything to do with it."

Adelia cleared her throat, gulping back the extra helping of guilt she'd just been served. It was enough to take care of any appetite she might have had for the rest of the day. "I know," she said, her mouth forming the words without her permission. "I know you'll be fine too. One day you'll find someone else and forgive your father. You'll see."

"Are you applying for the job?" Ricky asked, chuckling. He reached for the pen.

"Yes!"

His eyes jolted back to hers, the pen flew off the table. "What?"

The two bent down at the same time, reaching for the pen. Their heads banged against each other. The second bump was fingers reaching out. A shock bolted through them on contact, sending goosebumps in both directions.

"I got it," Ricky said, sitting back up, pen grasped firmly in hand. "What were you saying?"

Adelia's head cocked to the side, her eyes taking in every movement the man in front of her made. The power of the shock she'd received still tingled through her fingers, as if somehow it had entered her blood stream sending an arrow directly to her heart. "The job," she managed to say in no more than a whisper. "I want to work here."

Her hand rubbed over her chest, feeling the irregular beating of her heart. That was impossible. A faerie couldn't feel... love.

CHAPTER ELEVEN

"So it is your testimony that you fell in love with a mortal?" the sole female on the Consillium's panel asked.

"Yes," Adelia answered.

Quissum yawned. "Is this tale finished yet?"

"Almost," Adelia answered. If this had been a month ago, she wouldn't have batted an eye at the faerie for his actions. Now, she knew his yawns were meant to mock her. Faeries didn't get tired; they didn't sleep; and they most definitely didn't need to yawn.

"Shall we bring the others implicated in your story in for questioning? Perhaps Junapree?" Quissum suggested.

Adelia was sure the Consillium had no desire to listen to any more testimony than they needed to. This line of questioning was a ploy. They were blackmailing her. The longer she lingered over the words, the worse the conspiracy theories were that formed in her mind. She shook her head. "No."

"No?" the female asked.

"They aren't involved, directly," Adelia answered. "I take full responsibility. If anything, Junapree tried to stop things from progressing as they did. When he returned, I told him I hadn't found a match for Ricky. I said I needed more time."

"And what did he do?" Quissum asked.

"He brought me back," Adelia explained. "He turned me in. He's the only reason I am here before you now."

"Perhaps, but he was involved in the original mix-up. He does bear some of the blame for the events as they unfolded," Quissum argued, glancing down at his paperwork as if considering the proper direction for justice to take.

"If I may," Adelia stated. "We believe that magic has an all-knowing presence behind it. We trust that it knows what it is doing. Should we not also consider the possibility that this was all orchestrated?"

"Are you suggesting that the events of the past few days were designed by fate?" Quissum asked. "That somehow they could not be avoided?"

"Yes," Adelia admitted. "I am."

"An interesting theory," Quissum stated. "We'll take a moment to consider the testimony you have presented."

Deliberation wasn't at all what she had expected. They merely cupped their hands in front of their mouths and whispered to each other, their tones not quite loud enough to hear the entire conversation, but high enough to pick up bits and pieces. She was in trouble. This wasn't anything that was going to end well. Of course, that had been obvious since the moment of her return.

Adelia bit her bottom lip - a poor attempt at distraction. A stinging sensation in her eyes grew with every attempt to hold back tears begging for release. Crying in front of the Consillium was the worst thing she could have done. She'd been compromised. There was no doubt about it. Emotions had crept in like a low rolling fog, before she knew it she had been fully engulfed by the mist, unable to see the path that led back to the life she had been living.

"A decision has been reached!" Quissum announced. A copper coloured metal plate hanging behind him vibrated, alternating between several different, yet equally annoying tones. It was a siren alerting all to judgement having been made and passed. Only the sentencing remained - her fate was already sealed.

Adelia's hands covered her ears, the deafening noises crippling her mind. All she could do was pray it would end as quickly as it had started. A realization of what was to come mortified her. With the panel now standing, she could see their expressions. Their faces reflected nothing short of disgust, anger and disappointment. Was it her imagination? The ringing ceased. Replacing it was a cruel laughter that seeped through the walls. Every second she remained planted in that spot was utter humiliation. Still, she couldn't run or move for that matter. The final decision of the Consillium needed to be read aloud.

"Adelia, faerie of the cupid department," A voice bellowed, one she hadn't heard before. It was strong, yet meek and neither male nor female. "It has been unanimously agreed that you have broken a sacred law. Punishment for such behaviour is banishment from the faerie world. You will be stripped of your wings, magic and memories and returned to the world of men immediately."

Adelia's legs gave way, she fell to her knees. There was no way to prepare for such a moment, even if she had known it was coming. Her hands crossed over her heart, feeling it beat faster than ever before. Her life as a faerie was over.

The ringing returned. This time she barely heard the deafening noises. She blinked at a flash of bright light, no doubt a picture had been taken for the wall of the damned. She was officially a criminal.

CHAPTER TWELVE

Junapree's hands shook as he drew back the arrow in his bow. His eyes lingered a little too long on his mortal subject. Enough time had already been wasted watching her from a loft no longer used. Perched above, he was a frozen statue, meant to be nothing more than a decoration - one no one could see. No one, that was, except a tiny mouse that had taken up a front row seat beside him. Its liquid black eyes were glued to the people below, whiskers twitching. Tiny paws similar to hands held a piece of food it had found and stashed away before cleaners had finished their job the evening before. This was dinner and a movie.

Junapree's lips curled up, his eyes focused on the tiny rodent's shiny fur. The arrow whistled through the air. It was done. His fingers came together, preparing to snap him back home. He stopped short, his teeth grinding against each other loud enough to frighten his tiny friend away. Glancing back was a mistake he couldn't stop himself from making.

He sighed. This was his punishment. This was the Consillium's way of knowing he hadn't been effected by emotions the same way as Adelia had. It was done, but he wasn't sure he hadn't been touched by the world of man or by his faerie friend he'd never forget.

He felt something move from inside as he watched Ricky take Adelia's waist, pulling her close and planting his lips firmly on hers. Their embrace was tender and warm. It was one he had seen numerous times before, yet this time it made him feel sick. The longer he watched, the more painful the pangs ripped him apart. It didn't make sense for him to remain, at the same time he couldn't bring himself to leave.

He wasn't an expert on mortal emotions, no faerie was. Was this jealousy? Was this love? Reasonable thought dictated it was neither, but rather a curiosity. If magic taught anything, it was that there were somethings that couldn't be explained. This had to be one of those things. His thumb and finger pressed together, dust floating down to the crowd below.

"Goodbye, Adelia," he whispered, finishing the words before appearing back in the travelling room a realm away.

Other than the odd strange glance here or there, everything was as it had been. Junapree fought his way through crowds returning from their jobs for the day to the problem department. He snapped his fingers, a report of his performance appearing in the other hand. It landed with a thump on the dwarf's desk.

"It's done," Junapree stated.

"No problems then?" Eelbright asked.

"None," Junapree stated.

"Have a seat," the dwarf ordered, reaching into a desk drawer. His hand retrieved a bottle of yellow liquid. "Shall we have a drink?"

"My goodness," Eelbright cooed. "Where did you get your hands on dandelion nectar? It's a rather rare commodity with the way the world of men have been destroying them."

"Ah," the dwarf answered. "I have my sources. It is hard to come by, but not impossible. Shall we toast to Adelia?"

Junapree's gaze locked on the dwarf's. "Adelia? Tell me, what is to become of her?"

Eelbright pursed her lips together. "Nothing," she said in a matter-of-fact tone. "She has the identity that was given her as a cover intact, including the property and we even added memories of a wonderful life. I expect she will have children, grow old and die never knowing a thing about her life as a faerie. Then her soul will be added to the pool of those waiting to be reborn."

"You did a good job today," the dwarf praised. "I have to admit, I thought you might have been touched by them."

"By them," Junapree echoed. "You mean by the world of men."

"Yes," the dwarf said, finishing off the yellow drink and pouring another.

"I may be way off-base, but," Junapree started, "weren't we all once mortal?"

Eelbright held up her glass. "You are a smart one, aren't you?" she said, exchanging glances with the dwarf. "It's true. Faeries are merely mortals who have been touched by magic. Once exposed to the possibilities, it is hard to go back. Each of us willingly gave up our lives in the world of men to be here."

"There was a price to pay, though," Junapree stated.

"It is an equal trade off, magic for emotions," the dwarf answered. "No one can have both. I suppose it is too dangerous... rather like handing a loaded gun to a drunk man who thinks his wife is having an affair. Odds are he is going to use it. Nothing good can come of it if he does."

"And that's why there are rules about coming too close to mortals?" Junapree questioned.

"It works both ways," Eelbright explained. "The grass is always greener on the other side. Both the magical and non-magical always want what they don't have. If we come too close to feelings, it is inevitable we would want to feel. That's what happened to Adelia."

"Shouldn't we be allowed to choose?" Junapree asked.

Eelbright laughed. "My dear," she said, "if we exposed ourselves to the world of men, they would all choose magic. I could name off all the emotions involved in the decision: greed; lust; envy; gluttony. Shall I continue?"

"Then we would all be faeries," Junapree said. "What's wrong with that? Those core emotions would be wiped out."

"You forget," Eelbright replied, "we are immortal and we do not reproduce. There are no faerie children. If every living person in the world of men became a faerie, there would be no more births. Souls would be trapped forever, unable to complete the cycle of reincarnation. Emotion would become a buried relic in a world long past."

"Understood," Junapree said with a waggle of his eyebrows. He gulped back the remainder of his drink.

"You are welcome to join this department," Eelbright offered. "We could use a faerie with your understanding of things."

"Perhaps in a decade or two," Junapree answered. "I'm only beginning in the position I have here. Rushing into a new one could be counterproductive."

"Always thinking," the dwarf chuckled. "I have a feeling you'll be moving up sooner than you think."

Junapree bowed his head before exiting. He headed straight for another assignment. At the late hour, there was barely a line up. His hand dove into the swirling magic, retrieving a message for his eyes only. One eyebrow raised as it opened. There was only one name. He traced his fingers over the letters. *ADELIA*.

He folded the paper, storing it in a pocket, knowing the second name would one day appear. Perhaps in a century or two, he'd be ready to give up magic to explore all that love had to offer. Until then, he knew exactly where she was. As long as she was happy, he had no need to interfere.

He pulled a second slip.

"George Pilper and Rosemarie DeCante, prepare to be shot through the heart. You two are about to fall in love."

The End

***

ABOUT THE AUTHOR

C.A. King is the recipient of several awards, including: The Hamilton Spectator Readers' Choice Award for 2017 Best Author; The Brant News Readers' Choice Award for 2017 Best Author; Readers' Favourite award in the short story/novella category; the 2017 SIBA Award for Best New Adult; and the 2017 SIBA Award for Best Novella. Currently residing in Brantford, Ontario Canada, she lives with her two sons. She began her writing career after the tragic loss of her parents and husband. Redirecting her emotions through writing became therapeutic in her battle with depression and in 2014 she decided to publish some of her works.

Other Titles from C.A. King

The Portal Prophecies

These great titles in C.A. King's The Portal Prophecies series are available now at most online book retailers:

A Keeper's Destiny

A Halloween's Curse

Frost Bitten

Sleeping Sands

Deadly Perceptions

Finding Balance

The prophecies are the key to their survival. Can they solve them in time?

Shattering the Effects of Time

Join the Shinning brothers, Jessie, Dezi and Pete as they set out on a quest to save their younger sister. No magic known to them or their friends has ever been able to reverse the grip of time. A few legends, however, exist mentioning ancient items that may hold the key to do exactly that.

This brand new series will take you on a search for the Fountain of Youth and Mermaids; a quest for the Holy Grail; a trip to visit Daryl the mountain guru, in the hunt for the Cinamani Stone; on a search for Ambrosia, the food of the Gods; and other adventures.

Surviving the Sins: Answering the Call

The prophecies are being rewritten. This time someone is using the seven deadly sins: Lust; Gluttony; Greed; Sloth; Wrath; Envy; and Pride, to unlock an ancient evil. The book falls into Jade's hands to answer destiny's call. Can she survive the sins?

Surviving the Sins: Pride

No one is safe when a witch's pride is at stake.

Prudance is back in Pewterclaw, and she isn't about to give up her prestigious status without a fight - especially not because of vampires. As an eighth-generation witch, she plans to do whatever it takes to stop the proposed new legislation from becoming law, including waking the dead for help.

Humility isn't in her vocabulary. With an ego spinning out of control and ancestral power at her fingertips, Prudance weaves a plot to keep Jade and Gavin separated. Will it be enough to satisfy the spirits she summoned?

When her pride costs more than she bargained for, someone has to pay the tab - but who will it be?

Surviving the Sins: Lust

What Mother doesn't know won't hurt her.

Lucinda has spent her entire existence running The Organization and looking after Mother's needs without complaint. That's about to change. A burning desire had manifested inside her - one she could no longer deny... Lust.

When Constable Safron Black shows up unexpected with news of an imprisoned God, Lucinda unravels. With power fuelling her passion, she'll do anything to make Morynx her mate.

****

Jade and her friends find themselves at a standstill. They have already failed to stop Pride from completing its task and they haven't located any victims for the other six sins. A strange fire in the municipal office puts them hot on the trail of what could be answers. Will they be in time to stop the dial from moving and further opening the way for Morynx?

When Leaves Fall: A Different Point of View Story

Ralph wakes up to what others only experience in a nightmare. Chained to a shed, he has no idea where he is, or who his captor is. His memories a blurred at best. As the days press on he finds himself experiencing a roller coaster of feelings. Hunger, thirst and pain become his only companions. Flashbacks of a happier time are all he has to keep him going. As his situation deteriorates, he finds himself doubting the very things he wants most - a family.

When Leaves Fall is a dramatic-thriller with a twist. Keep the tissue box close for the ending.

Tomoiya's Story

A Vampire Tale. She had a secret but she wasn't the only one who had something to hide.

Book I ~ Escape to Darkness

Book II ~ Collection Tears

Book III~ Coming Soon

Peach Coloured Daisies: A Cursed by the Gods Story

He couldn't die. An ancient curse meant she always did. This time, that was going to change - one way or another.

When Daisy's grandmother, her last living relative, passes away, she doesn't know where to turn. Things go from bad to worse when a local psychic tells her about a curse. Alone and confused, she ends up in front of her college professor's office, ready to cry her heart out in his arms.

Matt Demi might be the son of a God, but he's living the life of a cursed man. He's had to watch the woman he loves die on her twenty-first birthday countless times. Nothing he does seems to be able to affect the outcome. When she shows up at his office scared out of her wits by a psychic's prediction, he vows this time will be different.

With only three days, Matt will need to embrace a side of him he swore off long ago to save her, but will he lose himself in the process?

Flower Shields: A Four Horsemen Novel

Meet the four horsemen: Michael, Gabrielle, Uriel and Raphael. For centuries their job has been to guard the gates of hell, making sure they never open. Without the keys, there was never any real threat. That's about to change. There are rumours on the horizon that demon followers unearthed scrolls that explain exactly how to find the lost keys. This new battle is a race to see which side locates them first.

Michael couldn't care less about the love story behind how and why the world was created. In fact, nothing matters to him other than keeping the gates to hell closed. If one of the lost keys ever fell into the wrong hands, all humanity would be doomed. He's not going to let that happen - at any cost.

****

Tara's life is nothing short of a disaster. She's managed to flunk out of college with about the same amount of dignity as every relationship she's been in. The only constant in her life has been her love for flowers. When she's attacked at work, a stranger comes to her aid. Michael might be good-looking, but he's also arrogant, bossy and crazy. He's also her only chance to figure out who attacked her and why. Should she follow her heart and trust him - or listen to her head and run?

Miracles Not Included

A heartfelt romantic story about: life; love; loss; and learning to love again. If only life came with instructions and a warning label ~ Miracles Not Included.

****

Chris was born to be a writer. Even the smallest of details couldn't pass without notice, often becoming part of a plot for her next novel. The one thing she never saw coming was her husband's sudden illness.

Jason loved his wife from the moment they met. Nothing could ever change that - nothing except the death sentence he'd been handed - a terminal cancer diagnosis.

His story was ending: Hers was starting a new chapter and more than one miracle was needed to turn the page.

Twisted Tales of a Dead End Street

A paranormal mystery laced with comedic undertones: Twisted Tales of a Dead End Street.

Nine neighbours were invited to the mysterious dinner party at 9 Nine Street. Their host, the owner of the mansion, had more planned for the evening than just roast beef. When the secret of their quiet street was revealed, everything changed, blurring the lines between the tangible and the paranormal.

Was the number nine the difference between life and death? Would any of them survive long enough to uncover the truth? They would each soon find out this wasn't a simple case of who-done-it so much as one of what was being done and by whom.

www.ingramcontent.com/pod-product-compliance
Lightning Source LLC
Chambersburg PA
CBHW031857170626
46807CB00004B/1765